Dark Ways

By

Harriet Prescott Spofford

British Library Cataloguing-in-Publication Data
A catalogue record for this book is available from the
British Library

Harriet Elizabeth Prescott Spofford

Harriet Elizabeth Prescott Spofford was born on 3rd April 1835 in Calais, Maine, United States. She is now best known for her novels, poems and detective stories – a true pioneer of the American detective genre. When she was still a baby, Spofford's parents moved to Newburyport, Massachusetts, where she chose to stay for almost her entire life. Although she spent many of her winters in Boston and Washington D.C., Newburyport remained always close to Spofford's heart.

She attended the Putnam Free School in Newburyport and Pinkerton Academy in Derry, New Hampshire from 1853 to 1855. At Newburyport her prize essay on Hamlet drew the attention of Thomas Wentworth Higginson (a Unitarian minister, author, abolitionist, and soldier), who soon became her friend and gave Spofford much needed counsel and encouragement throughout her career. When Spofford was in her mid-twenties, her parents suffered from ill health, and of necessity she was set to work as a writer, sometimes labouring fifteen hours a day. She contributed to various Boston story papers for small fees, but her first major success came in 1859; this was Spofford's submission to *Atlantic Monthly* (a literary and cultural magazine) of a story about Parisian life, 'In a Cellar'. The magazine's editor, James Russell Lowell, first believed the story to be a translation and withheld it from publication. Reassured it was original, he eventually published it, and the narrative established her reputation.

After this success, Spofford became a welcome contributor to the chief periodicals of the United States, both of prose and poetry.

Spofford's fiction had very little in common with what was regarded as representative of 'the New England mind.' Her gothic romances were set apart by luxuriant descriptions and an unconventional handling of female stereotypes of the day. Her writing was ideal and intense in feeling, revelling in sensuous delights and material splendour. Nowhere was this more evident than, in 'Circumstance', an allegorical short story which takes place in the woods of Maine. In this tale, the protagonist comes into contact with the Indian Devil, forcing her to come to terms with her own life, sexuality and fears. By the end of the story, her husband shoots the Devil with his shotgun in one hand and their baby in the other while the 'true Indian Devils' destroy their home and town. When Wentworth Higginson asked Emily Dickinson whether she had read Spofford's work, Dickinson replied, 'I read Miss Prescott's 'Circumstance,' but it followed me in the dark, so I avoided her.' Other notable works include *The Thief in the Night* (1872), *The Servant Girl Question* (1881), *A Scarlet Poppy and Other Stories* (1894), and *The Fairy Changeling* (1910).

In 1865, at the age of thirty, the authoress married Richard S. Spofford, a Boston lawyer, and the couple resided on Deer Island overlooking the Merrimack River at Amesbury, a suburb of Newburyport. They lived here for the rest of their lives. Harriet Prescott Spofford died on 14th August 1921, aged eighty-six.

Dark Ways

"Tortured with winter's storms, and tossed with a tumultuous sea."

WHEN God's curse forsook my country, it fell on me. I had been young and heroic; I had fought well; what portion of the clock-work of Fate had been allotted me I had utterly performed. Twelve years ago I became a man and strove for my country's freedom; now she has attained her heights without me, and I -- what am I? A shapeless hulk, that stays in the shadow, and that hates the world and the people of the world, and verily the God above the world!

"Fight!" whispered Father Anselmo, the young priest, to me, at my last shrift; and fight I did. For from Italy's bosom I had drawn the strength of sword-arm, hip, and thigh; and I vowed to lose that arm and life and all that made life dear toward the trampling of oppressors from the sacred place.

My sun rose in storm, it continued in storm, -- why not so have set? Why not have died when swords swept their lightnings about me, when the glorious thunders of battle rolled around and sulphurous blasts enveloped, when the air was full of the bray of bugle and beat of drum, of shout and shriek, exultation and agony? Why not have gone with the crowd of souls reeking with daring and desire? Why, oh, why thus left alone to wither? Why still hangs that sun above me, yet wrapt and veiled and utterly obscured in thick, murk mists of sorrow and despair?

Peace! -- let me tell you my story.

Since Father Anselmo -- like all youth, whether under cowl, cap, or crown -- was a Liberal at heart, I had not wanted counsel; but when I had told him all my yearnings and aspirations, had bared to him the throbbings of my very thought, and he had replied in that one blessed word, I hastened away. There were none to whom I should say farewell; I was alone in the world. This wild blood of my veins ran in no other veins; I knew thoroughly the wide freedom of solitude; the sins and the virtues of my race, whatever they were, had culminated in me. As I looked back, that morning, the castle, planted in a dimple of its demesnes, old and gray and watched by purple peaks of Apennine, seemed to hide its command only under the mask of silence. The wood through which I went, with its alluring depths, the moss verdant in everlasting spring beneath my eager feet, each bough I lifted, the blossoms that blew their gales after, the bearded grasses that shook in the wind, all gave me their secret sigh; all the sweet land around, the distant hill, the distant shore, said, "Redeem me from my chains!" I came across a sylvan statue, some faun nestled in the forest: the rains had stained, frosts cracked, suns blistered it; but what of those? A vine covered with thorns and stemmed with cords had wreathed about it and bound it closely in serpent-coils. I stayed and tore apart the fetters till my hands bled, cut away the twisting branches, and set the god free from his bonds. Triumph rose to my lips, for I said, "So will I free my country!" Ah, there was my error, -- the shackling vines would grow again, and infold the marble image that had consecrated the forest-glooms; there is the flaw in all my work, -- I have shorn, but have never uprooted an evil. Youth is a fool; the young Titans cannot scale heaven, -- heaven, that, if what I live through be true, is ramparted round with tyrant lies! But is it true? Am I what I seem to myself? Did I fail in my purpose, in my will? Did Italy herself belie me? Did she, did she I loved, she I worshipped, she the woman to whom I gave all, for whom I sacrificed all, did she, too, forsake me? Ah, no! you will tell me Italy is free. But I did not free her! She waits only to put on in Venice her tiara. And for that other one, that fair Austrian woman, that devil whom I serve and adore, that yellow-haired witch who brewed her incantations in my holiest raptures, -- she did not then play me foul, and falsely feign love to win me to disgrace? May all the woes in Heaven's hands fall on her!

God! what have I said? That I should live to ban her with a word! Did I say it? Oh, but it was vain! Woe for her? No, no! all blessings shower upon her, sunshine attend her, peace and gladness dwell about her! Traitress though she were, I must love her yet; I cannot unlove her; I would take her into my heart, and fold my arms about her. -- Oh, I pray you do not look upon me with that mocking smile! Pity me, rather! pity this wretched heart that longs to curse God and die! -- Nay, I want not your idle words. Can good destroy? Can love persecute? I was a worm that turned. What then? Why not have crushed me to annihilation? Oh, no, not that! He took me up and shook me before the world, clipped me, and let me fall. I derisive Deity, -- why, the words give each other the lie!

Stop! Your sad eyes look as if you would go away, but for this infinite pity in you. What makes you pity me? Because I am shorn of my strength? because of all my fair proportions there is nothing left unshrivelled? because my body -- such as it is -- is racked with hourly and perpetual pain? because I die? For none of these? Truly, your judgments are inscrutable. For what then? Because, -- yet, no, that cannot be, -- because I bear a stubborn heart? because I will not bend my soul as He has bent my body? Partly, -- but you are witless! What else? Because I toss off a shield and buckler, you say. Because I will not lean upon a tower of strength. Because I will not throw myself on the tide of divine love, and trust myself to its course. It was that divine love, then, that tower of strength, that shield and buckler, that made m this thing you see. Tarpeia was enough. Away with your generalities! Go, go, you slave of the past!

Yet no, -- you have not gone? You believe what you say, -- I know with those eyes you cannot deceive. Ah, but I trusted her eyes once! Yet it gives you rest; -- your sorrows are not like mine, -- there *is* no rest for me. I cannot go and gather that balm of Gilead, -- I have no legs. I have as good as none. This wheel-chair and that dog of a turnkey are not the equipage for such a journey.

-- Ah, do not turn from me now! My railing is worse than my cursing, you feel indeed. Well, stay with me at least, and if it is twelve years since you shrived me at first, perhaps you shall shrive me at last, -- for I doubt if I am ever brought out to this sunshine again, if I do not die in the prison-damps tonight, -- and you, with all your change, are Father Anselmo, I think. -- Stay, I will confess to you, confess this. Man! man! this infinite pity of your soul for mine throws a light on my dark ways: God's curse has fallen on me through man's curse, why not God's love through man's love? Anselmo, though you became priest, and I went to become hero, we were children together; I was dear to you then; I am so still, it seems. In your love let me find the love of that Heaven I have defied. -- Stay, friend, yet another word. If man's love can be so great, what can God's love be? That which I said I said in desperation; in very truth, that peace hangs like an unattainable city in the clouds before my soul's vision, that love like a broad river flowing through the lands, an atmosphere bathing the worlds, the subtile essence and ether of space in which the farthest star pursues its course, -- why, then, should it escape me, the mote? Oh, when the world turned from me, I sought to flee thither! I sighed for the rest there! Wretched, alone, I have wept in the dark and in the light that I might go and fling myself at the heavenly feet. But, do you see? sin has broken down the bridge between God and me. Yet why, then, is sin in the world, -- that scum that rises in the creation and fermentation of good, -- why, but *as* a bridge on which to re-seek those shores from which we wander? Man, I do repent me, -- in loving you I find

God. And you call that blasphemy! -- Nay, go, indeed, my friend! So humble, you are not the man for me. I can talk to the winds: they, at least, do not visit me too roughly.

These are thy tears, Anselmo? Thou a priest, yet a man? Still with me? Yet thou wilt have to bear with wayward moods, -- scorn now, quiet then. I am a tetchy man; I am an old man, too, though but just past thirty. -- So! I thank God for thee, dear friend!

Anselmo, look out on this scene below us here, as we sit on our lofty battlement. Not on the turrets of the loopholes, the grates and spikes, or all the fortified horror, -- but on the earth. It is fair earth, though not Italy; this is a mountain-fortress; here are all the lights and shadows that play over grand hill-countries, and yonder are fields of grain, where the winds and sunbeams play at storm, and a little hamlet's sheltered valley. Doubtless there are towers, besides, half hidden in the hills. It is Austria: slaves tread it, and tyrants drain it, it is true, -- but the wild, free gypsies troop now and then across it, and though no fiction of law supports a claim they would scorn to make, they use it so that you would swear they own it. Do you see how this iron reticulation of social rule and custom and force makes a scaffolding on which this tameless race build up their lives? I watch them often. Each country has its compensations. Anselmo, this first made me tremble in my petty defiance, -- I, an ephemera of May, defying the dominations of eternity! -- Not so, -- not too lowly; I also am, and each limitation of life is as well, a domination of eternity. But I saw that it was no purpose of God to have destroyed Italy; when men in weakness and wantonness suffered their liberties to be torn from them, suffered themselves to become enslaved, there was compensation in that their sons had chance for heroic growth; they might, in efforts for freedom, create virtues that, born to freedom, they would never have known. I, too, had my field; I lost it; my enemy was myself. But when I think of her -- Ay, there it is! Do not let me think of her! I become mad, when I think of her! -- At least, allow me this: God's ways are dark. Not that? Not even that? I needed what I have? If my ambitions, my passions, my will, had ruled, my soul would have remained null? Ah, friend, and is that so much the worse? It is the soul that aches! -- I am a man of the people, a man who acts, -- I *was*, I mean, -- not a man who thinks; and all your subtleties of word perchance entrap me. I am not wary when you come to logic. See! I surrender point after point. I shall be dead soon, you know; when this morning's sun shall have set, when the moon shall hold the night in fee, I shall depart, -- wing up and away; -- is it, that, my body already dead, my mind sickens and dies with it, bit after bit, and so I yield, and attest, that, without the agony of my life, death had failed to burst my soul's husk? Oh, for I was born of an earthy race, blood ran thick in our veins, we were sensuous and passionate, the breath and steam of pleasure stifled our brains, and our filmy eyes could not see heaven. Yes, yes, I needed it all; but, friend, it is pitiful.

I like to sit here in the sun. It is only a twelvemonth, of all my long years' imprisonment, that this has been allowed me. I like to sleep in it, like any wild creature, -- the lizard, a mere reptile, -- the bird, a hindered soul. To lie thus, weak as I am, but pillowed and warmed by the searching genial rays, seems such comfort, when I think of the bed I once had on the rack! This little slumber from which I wake revives me. I feared not to find you, and did not unclose my eyes at once. It was good in you to come, Anselmo; it must have been at risk of much.

You ask me to speak of my life since I went away on that morning of your command, -- to reconcile the hostile acts, to gather the scattered reports. Hear it all!

You know my wealth was equal to my demand. I used it; before six months were over, I was the life and soul of those who must needs be conspirators. They saw that I was earnest, that my sacrifices were real; they trusted me. Soon the movement had become general; all the smothered elements of national life were convulsed and throbbing under the crust of tyranny.

How proud and glad was I that morning after our victory! I saw great Italy, beautiful Italy, once more put on her diadem; I beheld the future prospect of one broad, free land, barriered by Alps and set impregnably in summer seas, storied seas, keys of the West and East. We embraced each other as brothers of this glorious nation, ancient Rome risen from trance; as we walked the streets, we sand; Milan was turbulent with gladness; no gala-day was ever half so bright; the very spires appeared to spring in the white radiance of their flames up a deeper heaven; the sun stayed at perpetual dawn for us. Walking along, jubilant and daring, at length we paused in a square where a fountain dashed up its column of sunshine, and laved our hands. By Heaven! We forgot independence, Italy, freedom; we were crazed with success and hope; it seemed that the stream was Austrian blood! Then, in the midst of all, I looked up, -- and on a balcony she stood. A fair woman, with hair like shredded light, her great blue eyes wide and full and of intense dye, her nostril distended with pride, and fear and hate of us, -- but on the full lips, ripe with crimson bloom, juicy and young and fresh, on those Love lay. The others wound forward, -- I with them, yet apart; and my eyes became fixed on hers. Then I lifted my cap with its tricolor. She did not return the courtesy, but stood as if spellbound, one hand threading back the straying hair, the lips a little parted; suddenly she turned to fly, that hand upraised to the casement's side, and still, as she looked back, the beautiful eyes on mine. My companions had preceded me; we were alone in the square; she wavered as she stood, then tore a rose from her bosom, kissed it deep into its heart, and tossed it to me.

"Let all its petals be joys!" I said, and she vanished.

Oh, friend, the leaves have fallen, the rose is dead! Look! I have kept it through all, -- sear leaf and withered spray!

That night we danced; and the Austrian girl was there. They told me she was exiled, and that she loved liberty; no one told me she was a spy. I saw her swim along the dance, the white satin of her raiment flashing perpetual interchange of lustrous and obscure, the warm air playing in the lace that fell like the spray of the fountain round her golden hair and over her pearly shoulder; grace swept in all her motions, beauty crowned her, she seemed the perfect pitch of womanhood.

Still she swims along the lazy line with indolent pleasure, still floats in dreamy waltz-circles perchance, still bends to the swaying tune as the hazel-branch bends to the hidden treasure, -- but as for me, my dancing days are over.

By-and-by it was I with whom she danced, whose hand she touched, on whom she leaned. I wondered if there were any man so blest; I listened to her breath, I watched her cheek, our eyes met, and I loved her. The music grew deeper, more impassioned; we stood and listened to it, -- for she danced then no more, -- our hearts beat time to it, the wind wandering at the casement played in its measure; we said no words, but now and then each sought the other's glance, and, convicted there, turned in sudden shame away. When I bade her good-night, which I might never have done but

that the revel broke, a great curl of her hair blew across
my lips. I was bold, -- I was heated, too, with this half-
secret life of my heart, this warm blood that went leaping
so riotously through my veins, and yet so silently, -- I
took my dagger from my belt and severed the curl. See,
friend! will you look at it? It is like the little gold snakes
of the Campagna, is it not? each thread, so fine and fair,
a separate ray of light: once it was part of her! See how it
twists round my hand! Haste! haste! let me put it up, lest
I go mad! -- Where was I?

I busied myself again in the work to be done;
because of our victory we must not rest; once more all
went forward. I saw the Austrian woman only from a
window, or in a church, or as she walked in the gardens,
for many days. Then the times grew hotter; I left the
place, and lived with stern alarums; and thither she also
came. I never sought what sent her. She was with the
wounded, with the dying. Then the need of her was past,
and she and all the others took their way. At length that
also came to an end.

We were in Rome, -- and thither, some time
previously, she had gone.

One night, our business for the day was over, our
plans for the morrow laid, our messages received, our
messengers despatched, and those who had been
conspirators and now bade fair to be saviours were
sleeping. Sleep seemed to fold the world; each bough and
twig was silent in repose; the spectral moonlight itself

slept as it bathed the air. I alone wandered and waked. With me there were too many cares for rest; work kept me on the alert; to court slumber at once was not easy after the nervous tension of duty. I was torn, too, with conflicting feelings: half my soul went one way in devotion to my country, half my soul swerved to the other as I thought of the Austrian woman. I grew tired of the streets and squares; something that should be fragrant and bowery attracted me. I mounted on the broken water-god of a dry bath and leaped a garden-wall.

No sooner was I there than I knew why I had come. This was her garden.

Heart of Heaven! how all things spoke of her! How the great white roses hung their doubly heavy heads and poured their perfume out to her! how the sprays shivered as I spoke the name she owned! how the nightingales ceased for a breath their warbling as she rustled down a fragrant path and met me! All her hair was swept back in one great mass and held by an ivory comb; a white cloak wrapped her white array; she was jewelless and stripped of lustre; she was like pearl, milky as a shell, white as the moonlight that followed in her wake.

"You breathed my name, -- I came," she said.

"Pardon!" I replied. "I heard the fountains dash and the nightingales sing, and I but came for rest under the spell."

"And have you found it?"

"I have found it."

We remained silent then, while floods of passion gathered and lay darkly still in our hearts. No, no! I know now that it was not so; yet I will tell it, tell it all, as I thought it then.

She did not stir; indeed, she had such capability of rest, that, had I not spoken, she would never have stirred, it may be. She knew that my glance was upon her; for herself, she looked at the broad lilies that grew at her feet, and listened to the melody that seemed to bubble from a thousand throats with interfluent sound upon the night. It was her repose that soothed me: moulded clay is not so calm, the marble rose of silence not half so beautifully folded to dreamful rest, so lovely and so still no garden-statue could have been; the cool, soft night infiltrated its tranquillity through all her being.

As we stood, the nightingales gave us capricious pause; one alone, distant and clear, fluted its faint piping like the phantom of the finished strain. Another sound broke the air and floated alone on this too delicious accompaniment: music, fine and far. Some other lover sang to her his serenade. The voice in its golden sonority rose and crept toward her with persuading sweetness, winding through all the alleys and hovering over the plots of greenery with a tranquil strength, as if such song

were but the natural spirit of the night, or as if the soul
of the broad calm and silence itself had taken voice.

"Thy beauty, like a star
Whose life is light,
Shines on me from afar,
And on the night.

"Each midnight blossom bends
With sweetest weight,
And to thy casement sends
Its fragrant freight.

"Each air that faintly curls
About thy nest
Its daring pinion furls
Within thy breast.

"The night is spread for thee,
The heavens are wide,
And the dark earth's mystery
Is magnified.

"For thee the garden waits,
The hours delay,
The fountains toss their jets

Of shimmering spray.

"Then leave thy dim delight
In dreams above,
Come forth, and crown the night
With her I love!"

She listened, but did not lift her head or suffer the change of a fold; then there came the tinkle of the strings that embalmed the tune, and the singer's steps grew soundless as he left the street. A new phantasm crept upon me. What right had any other man to sing to her his love-songs? Did she not live, was not her beauty created, her soul given, for me? Did not the very breath she drew belong to me? My voice, hoarse and husky, disturbed the stillness, my eyes flamed on her.

"Do you love that man who sang?" I murmured.

"Signor, I love you," she said.

Then we were silent as before, but she stood no longer alone and opposite. One passionate step, an outstretched arm, and her head on my bosom, my lips bent to hers.

All the nightingales burst forth in choral redundance of song, all the low winds woke and fainted again through the balmy boughs, all the great stars bent out of heaven to shed their sweet influences upon us.

It seemed to me that in that old palace-garden life began, my memory went out in confused joy. I held her, she was mine! mine, mine, in life and for eternity! Fool! it was I who was hers! Man, you are a priest, and must not love. I, too, was sworn a priest to my country. So we break oaths!

O moments of swift bliss, why are you torture to remember? Let me not think how the night slipped into dawn as we roamed, how pale gold filtered through the darkness and bleached the air, how bird after bird with distant chirrup and breaking tune announced the day. She left me, and as well it might be night. I wound a strange way home. I questioned if it were the dream of a fevered brain; I wondered, would she remember when next she saw me? None met with me that day; I forgot all. With the night I again waited in the garden. In vain I waited; she came no more. I waxed full of love's anger, I crushed the tendril and the vine, I wandered up and down the walks and cursed these thorns that tore my heart. As I went, an angle of the shrubbery allured; I turned, and lo! full radiance from open doors, and silvery sounds of sport. I leaned against the ilex, lost in shadow, and watched her as she stirred and floated there before me in the light. She seemed to carry with her an atmosphere of warmth and brilliance; all things were ordered as she moved; one throng melted before her, another followed. By-and-by she stood at the long casement to seek acquaintance with the night. Constantly I thought to meet her eye, and I would not reflect that she saw only dusk and vacancy. Then indignantly I stepped from the ilex and confronted her. A low, glad cry escapes her lips, she holds her arms toward me and would cross the sill, when a voice constrains her from within. It is he, the accursed Neapolitan.

"Signor," she says, "a vampire flitted past the dawn."

Dawn indeed was breaking. The man still stood there when she left him, and still looked out; his eyes lay on me, and irate and motionless I returned their gaze. One by one her guests departed; with a last threatening glance, he, too, withdrew. I plunged into the silent places again, and waited now, assured that she would come. The constellations paled, and still I was alone. Then I wandered restlessly again, and, winding through thickets of leaf-distilled perfume, I came where just above a balcony, and almost beyond reach from it, a light burned dimly in one narrow window. I did not ask myself why I did it, but in another moment I had clambered to the place, and standing there, I bent forward to my right, pulled away the tangle of ivy that filled half the niche, and was peering in.

"What is that?" said a voice I knew, with its silvery echo of the South, the accursed Neapolitan's.

"It is the owl that builds in the recess, and stirs the ivy," she replied.

"Haste!" said a third, -- "the day breaks."

She was sitting at a low table, writing; Pia, the old nurse, stood behind her chair; the oil was richly scented that she burned; the single light illumined only her, and covered with her shadow the low ceiling, -- a shadow that seemed to hang above her like a pall ready to fall from ghostly fingers and smother her in its folds; the others lounged about the room and waited on her pen, in gloom they, their faces gleaming from that dusk demoniacly. It was a concealed room, entered by secret ways, unknown to others than these.

When she had written, she sealed.

"There is no more to await. Adieu," she said.

"It is some transfer of property, some legal paper, some sale, some gift," I said to myself, as I watched them take it and depart. Then she was alone again. I saw her start up, pace the narrow spot, -- saw her stand and pull down the masses, so interspersed with golden light, that crowned her head, and look at them wonderingly as they overlay her fingers, -- then saw those fingers clasped across the eyes, and the lips part with a sigh that, prolonged and deepened, grew to be a groan, -- while all the time that shadow on the ceiling hovered and fluttered and grew still, till it seemed the cluster of

Eumenides waiting to pounce on its prey. In another pause I had taken the perilous step, had hung by the crumbling rock, the rending vine, had entered and was beside her. A cold horror iced her face; she warned me away with her trembling hands.

"What have you seen?" she said.

"You, O my love, in grief."

"And no more?"

"I have seen you give a letter to the Neapolitan, who departs to-morrow with the little Viennois, -- perhaps to your friends at home."

"And that is all?"

"That is all."

"I have no friends at home. To whom, then, could the letter be?"

"How should I divine?"

"It was for the Austrian Government! Now love me, if you dare!"

"And do you suppose I did not know it?"

"Then is your love for me but a shield and mask?"

As I gazed in reply, my steady eyes, the soul that kindled my smile, my open arms, all must have asseverated for me the truth of my devotion.

"Still?" she said. "Still? And you can keep your faith to me and to Italy?"

What was this doubt of me, this stain she would have cast upon my honor? That armor's polish was too intense to sustain it; it rolled off like a cloud from heaven. Italy's fortunes were *my* fortunes; it was impossible for me to betray them; this woman I would win to wed them. How long, how long my blood had felt this thing in her! how long my brain had rebelled! In a proud innocence, I stood with folded arms, and could afford to smile.

"Stay!" she said again, after our mute gaze, and laying her hand upon my arm. "You shall not love me in vain, you shall not trust me for nothing. Your cause is mine to-day. That is the last message I send to Vienna."

And then I believed her.

The light, slanting up, crept in and touched the brow of an ideal bust of Mithras which she had invested with her faintly-faded wreath of heliotropes; their fragrance falling through the place already made the atmosphere more rich than that of chest of almond-wood, -- this perfume that is like the soul of the earth itself exhaled to the amorous air. Behind an alabaster shrine she lighted a holy-taper, slowly to waste and pale in the spreading day. We went to the window, where among the ivy-nooks day's life was just astir with gaudy wings.

"All will be seeking you, and yet you cannot go," she said.

"Why can I not go?"

"It is broad morning."

"And what of that?"

"One thing. You shall not compromise yourself, going from the house of an Austrian woman and worse!"

She was too winningly imperious to fail. I delayed, and together we looked out on the rosy sky.

"Come down," she said at last, "and on an arbor-moss the sun shall drowse you, the flower-scents be your opiates, the birds your lullaby, and I your guard."

We went, and, wandering again through the garden-paths, she brushed the dew with her trailing festal garments, and plucked the great blue convolvuli to crown her forehead. Soon, on a plot of Roman violets, screened by tall trees and trellises, we breakfasted. One might have said that the cloth was laid above giant mushroom-stems, the service acorn-cups and calices of milky blooms; golden was the honey-comb we broke, manna was our bread; she caught the water in her hand from the fountain and pledged me, and swift as sunshine I bent forward and prevented the thirsty lips. Then she laid my head on her shoulder, with her cool finger-tips she stroked the temples and soothed the lids, they fell and closed on the vision bending above me, -- loveliness like painting, pallor that was waxen, yellow tresses wreathed with azure stars, eyes that caught the hue again and absorbed all Tyrian dyes.

The plash and bubble of waters swooned dreamily about my ears, and far off it seemed I heard the wild, sad songs of her native land, that now in tinkling tune, and now in long, slow rise and fall of mellow sound, swathed me with sweet satiety to dreamless rest.

The sun stole round and rose above the screen of trees at last and woke me. I was alone, the silent statues looked on me, the breath of the dark violets crushed by my weight rose in shrouding incense. I lifted myself and searched for her, and asked why I must needs believe each hour of joy a dream, -- then went and cooled my brow in the lucent basin at hand, and waited till she came, in changed raiment, and gliding toward me as the Spirit of Noon might have come. She led me in, well, refreshed, and in the cool north rooms of the palace the warm hours of the day slipped like beads from a leash. It scarcely seemed her fingers that touched the harp to tune, but as if some herald of sirocco, some faint, hot breeze, had brushed between the strings. It scarcely seemed her voice that talked to me, but something distant as the tone in a sad sea-shell. What I said I knew not; I was in a maze, bewildered with bliss; I only knew I loved her, I only felt my joy.

She told me many things: stories of her mountain-home, in distant view of the old fortress of Hellberg, -- this is the fortress of Hellberg, Anselmo, -- of her youth, her maidenhood, her life in Vienna, her lovers in Venice, her health, that had sent her finally there where we sat together.

"I thought it sad," she said at length, "when they exiled me, so to say, from Vienna and all my gay career there because Venice, with its water-breaths, might heal my attainted health, -- and sadder when the winter bade me leave night-tides and gondolas and repair to Rome. Now spring has come, and all the hills are blue with these deep violets, the very air is balm, the year is at flood, and life at what seems its height is perfected with you."

"But you love that land you left?" I replied, after a while, and lifting her face to meet my gaze.

"Love it? Oh, yes! You love your land as you love a person in whose veins and yours kindred blood runs, because it is hardly possible to do otherwise. The land gave me life, that is all; I never knew till lately that it was anything to be thankful for. It is not sufficiently a *country* to kindle enthusiasm; it has no national life, you know, -- is an automaton put through its motions by paid and cunning mechanists. I thought it right to obey orders and serve it. But now *you* are my country, -- I serve only you."

It was easy so to pass to my own hopes, to my own life, to my land, the land to which I had vowed the last drop of blood in my gift. Her eyes beamed upon me, smiles rippled over her face, she clasped me now and then and sealed my brow with kisses. Soon I left her side and strode from end to end of the long *salon*, speaking eagerly of the future that opened to Italy. I told her how the beautiful corpse lay waiting its resurrection, and how the Angel of Eternal Life hovered with spreading wings above, ready to sound his general trump. My pulses beat like trip-hammers, and as I passed a mirror I saw myself white with the excitement that fired me.

"You are wild with your joyous emotion," she said, coming forward and clinging round me. "Your eyes flame from depths of darkness. What, after all, is Italy to you, that your blood should boil in thinking of her wrongs? These people, for whom in your terrible magnanimity, I feel that you would sacrifice even me, to-morrow would turn and rend you!"

"No, no!" I answered. "All things but you! You, you, are before my country!"

The tears filled her large, serious eyes, her lips quivered in melancholy smile, as sunshine plays with shower over autumn woodlands. Was I not right? Right, though the universe declare me wrong! I would do it all again; if she loved me, she had authority to be first of all in my care; in love lie the highest duties of existence.

I had forgotten the subject on which we spoke; I was thinking only of her, her beauty, her tenderness, and the debt of deathless devotion that I owed her. It was otherwise in her thought; she had not dropped the old thread, but, looking up, resumed.

"It is, then, an idea that you serve?"

Brought back from my reverie, "Could I serve a more worthy master?" I asked.

"You do not particularly love your countrymen, nine-tenths of whom you have never seen? You do not particularly hate the hostile race, nine-tenths of whom you have never seen?"

"Abstractly, I hate them. Kindliness of heart prevents individual hatred, and without kindliness of heart in the first place there can be no pure patriotism."

"And for the other part. What do you care for these men who herd in the old tombs, raise a pittance of vetch, and live the life of brutes? what for the lazzaroni of Naples, for the brigands of Romagna, the murderers of the Appenine? Nay, nothing indeed. It is, then, for the land that you care, the mere face of the country, because it entombs myriad ancestors, because it is familiar in its every aspect, because it overflows with abundant beauty. But is the land less fair when foreign sway domineers it? do the blossoms cease to crowd the gorge, the mists to fill it with rolling color? is the sea less purple around you, the sky less blue above, the hills, the fields, the forests, less lavishly lovely?"

"Yes, the land is less fair," I said. "It is a fair slave. It loses beauty in the proportion of difference that exists between any two creatures, -- the one a slave of supple symmetry and perfect passivity, the other a daring woman who stands nearer heaven by all the height of her freedom. And for these people of whom you speak, first I care for them because they *are* my countrymen, -- and next, because the idea which I serve is a purpose to raise them into free and responsible agents."

"Each man does that for himself; no one can do it for another."

"But any one may remove the obstacles from another's way, scatter the scales from the eyes of the blind, strip the dead coral from the reef."

She took yellow honeysuckles from a vase of massed amethyst and began to weave them in her yellow hair, -- humming a tune, the while, that was full of the subtilest curves of sound. Soon she had finished, and finished the fresh thought as well.

"Do you know, my own," she said, "the men who begin as hierophants of an idea are apt to lose sight of the pure purpose, and to become the dogged, bigoted, inflexible, unreasoning adherents of a party? All leaders of liberal movements should beware how far they commit themselves to party-organizations. Only that man is free. It is easier to be a partisan then a patriot."

I laughed.

"Lady, you are like all women who talk politics, however capable they may be of acting them. You immediately beg the question. We are speaking of patriotism, not of partisanship."

"You it was who forsook the subject. You know nothing about it; you confess that it is with you merely a blind instinct; you cannot tell me even what patriotism is."

"Stay!" I replied. "All love is instinct in the germ. Can you define the yearnings that the mother feels toward her child, the tie that binds son to father? Then you can define the sentiment that attaches me to the land from whose breast I have drawn life. The love of country is more invisible, more imponderable, more inappreciable than the electricity that fills the air and flows with perpetual variation from pole to pole of the earth. It is as deep, as unsearchable, as ineffable as the power which sways me to you. It is the sublimation of other affection. A portion of you has always gone out into the material spot where you have been, a portion of that has entered you, your past life is entwined with river and shore. You become the country, and the country becomes a part of God. Those who love their country, love the vast abstraction, can almost afford not to love God. She is a beneficence, she is a shield, something for which to do and die, something for worship, ideal, grand; and though the sky is their only roof, the earth their only bed, affluent are they who have a land! Passion rooted deeply as the foundations of the hills: a man may adore one woman, but in adoring his land the aggregation of all men's love for all other women overwhelms him and accentuates to a fuller emotion. It is unselfish, impersonal, sheer sentiment clarified at its white heat from all interest and deceit, the noblest joy, the noblest sorrow. Bold should they be, and pure as the priests who bore the ark, that dare to call themselves patriots. And those, Lenore, who live to see their country's hopeless ruin, plunge into a sadness at heart that no other loss can equal, no remaining blessing mitigate, -- neither the devotion of a wife nor the perfection of a child. You have seen exiles from a lost land? Pride is dead in them, hope is dead, ambition is dead, joy is dead. Tell me, would you choose me to suffer the personal loss of love and you, a loss I could hide in my aching soul, or to bear those black marks of gall and melancholy which forever overshadow them in widest grief and gloom?"

She had sunk upon a seat, and was looking up at me with a pained unwavering glance, as if in my words she foresaw my fate.

"You are too intense!" she cried. "Your tones, your eyes, your gestures, make it an individual thing with you."

"And so it is!" I exclaimed. "I cannot sleep in peace, nor walk upon the ways, while these Austrian bayonets take my sunshine, these threatening approaching French banners hide the fair light of heaven!"

"Come," she said, rising. "Speak no more. I am tired of the burden of the ditty, dear; and it may do you such injury yet that already I hate it. Come out again into our garden with me. Dismiss these cares, these burning pains and rankling wounds. Be soothed by the cool evening air, taste the gorgeous quiet of sunset, gather peace with the dew."

So we went. I trusted her the more that she differed from me, that then she promised to love Italy only because *I* loved it. I told her my secret schemes, I took her advice on points of my own responsibility, I learned the joy of help and confidence in one whom you deem devotedly true. Finally we remained without speech, stood long heart to heart while the night fell around us like a curtain; her eyes deepened from their azure noon-splendor and took the violet glooms of the hour, a great planet rose and painted itself within them; again and again I printed my soul on her lips ere I left her.

At first, when I was sure that I was once more alone in the streets, I could not shake from myself the sense of her presence. I could not escape from my happiness, I was able to bring my thought to no other consideration. I reached home mechanically, slept an hour, performed the routine of bath and refreshment, and sought my former duties. But how changed seemed all the world to me! what air I breathed! in what light I worked! Still I felt the thrilling pressure of those kisses on my lips, still those dear embraces!

So days passed on. I worked faithfully for the purpose to which I was so utterly committed that let that be lost and I was lost! We were victorious; after the banner fell in Lombardy to soar again in Venice and sink, the Republic struggled to life; Rome rose once more on her seven hills, free and grand, child and mother of an idea, the idea of national unity, of independence and liberty from Tyrol to Sicily. My God! think of those dear people who for the first time said, "We have a country!"

Yet how could we have hoped then to continue? Such brief success dazzled us to the past. Piedmont had long since struck the key-note of Italy's fortunes. As Charles Albert forsook Milan and suffered Austria once more to mouth the betrayed land and drip its blood from her heavy jaws, till in a baptism of redder dye he absolved himself from the sin, -- so woe heaped on woe, all came to crisis, ruin, and loss, -- the Republic fell, Rome fell, the French entered.

Our names had become too famous, our heroic defence too familiar, for us to escape unknown: the Vascello had not been the only place where youth fought as the lioness fights for her whelps. Many of us died. Some fled. Others, and I among them, remained impenetrably concealed in the midst of our enemies. Weeks then dragged away, and months. New schemes chipped their shell. Again the central glory of the land might rise revealed to the nations. We never lost courage; after each downfall we rose like Antaeus with redoubled strength from contact with the beloved soil, for each fall plunged us farther into the masses of the people, into closer knowledge of them and kinder depths of their affection, and so, learning their capabilities and the warmth of their hearts and the strength of their endurance, we became convinced that freedom was yet to be theirs. Meanwhile, you know, our operations were shrouded in inscrutable secrecy; the French held Rome in frowning terror and subjection; the Pope trembled on his chair, and clutched it more franticly [sic] with his weak fingers: it was not even known that we, the leaders, were now in the city; all supposed us to be awaiting quietly the turn of events, in some other land. As if we ourselves were not events, and Italy did not hang on our motions! But, as I said, all this time we were at work; our emissaries gave us enough to do: we knew what spoil the robbers in the March had made, the decree issued in Vienna, the order of the day in Paris, the last word exchanged between the Cardinals, what whispers were sibilant in the Vatican; we mined deeper every day, and longed for the electric stroke which should kindle the spark and send princes and principalities shivered widely into atoms. But, friend, this was not to be. We knew one thing more, too: we knew at last that we also were watched, -- when men sang our songs in the echoing streets at night, and when each of us, and I, chief of all, renewed our ancient fame, and became the word in every one's mouth, so that old men blessed us in the way as we passed, wrapt, we had thought, in safe disguise, and crowds applauded. Thus again we changed our habits, our rendezvous, our quarters, and again we eluded suspicion.

There came breathing-space. I went to her to enjoy it, as I would have gone with some intoxicating blossom to share with her its perfume, -- with any band of wandering harpers, that together our ears might be delighted. I went as when, utterly weary, I had always gone and rested awhile with her I loved in the sweet old palace-garden: I had my ways, undreamed of by army or police or populace. There had I lingered, soothed at noon by the hum of the bee, at night by that spirit that scatters the dew, by the tranquillity and charm of the place, ever rested by her presence, the repose of her manner, the curve of her dropping eyelid, so that looking on her face alone gave me pleasant dreams.

Now, as I entered, she threw down her work, -- some handkerchief for her shoulders, perhaps, or yet a banner for those unrisen men of Rome, I said, -- a white silk square on which she had wrought a hand with a gleaming sickle, reversed by tall wheat whose barbed grains bent full and ripe to the reaper, and round the margin, half-pictured, wound the wild hedge-roses of Paestum. She threw it down and came toward me in haste, and drew me through an inner apartment.

"He has returned, they say," she said presently, -- mentioning the Neapolitan, -- "and it would be unfortunate, if you met."

"Unfortunate for *him*, if we met here!"

"How fearless! Yet he is subtler than the snake in Eden. I fear him as I detest him."

"Why fear him?"

"That I cannot tell. Some secret sign, some unspeakable intuition, assures me of injury through him."

"Dearest, put it by. The strength of all these surrounding leagues with their swarm does not flow through his wrist, as it does through mine. He is more powerless than the mote in the air."

"You are so confident!" she said.

"How can I be anything else than confident? The very signs in the sky speak for us, and half the priests are ours, and the land itself is an oath. Look out, Lenore! Look down on these purple fields that so sweetly are taking nightfall; look on these rills that braid the landscape and sing toward the sea; see yonder the row of columns that have watched above the ruins of their temple for centuries, to wait this hour; behold the heaven, that, lucid as one dome of amethyst, darkens over us and blooms in star on star; -- was ever such beauty? Ah, take this wandering wind, -- was ever such sweetness? And since every inch of earth is historic, -- since here rose glory to fill the world with wide renown, -- since here the heroes walked, the gods came down, -- since Oreads haunt the hill, and Nereids seek the shore" --

"Whereabout do Nereids seek the shore?" she archly asked.

"Why, if you must have data," I answered, laughing, "let us say Naples."

"What is that you have to say of Naples?" demanded a voice in the doorway, -- and turning, I confronted the Neapolitan.

She had started back at the abrupt apparition, and before she could recover, stung by rage and surprise I had replied, --

"What have I to say of Naples? That its tyrant walks in blood to his knees!"

A man, I, with my hot furies, to be intrusted with the commonwealth!

"I will trouble you to repeat that sentence at some day," he said.

"Here and now, if you will!" I uttered, my hand on my hilt.

"Thanks. Not here and now. It will answer, if you remember it *then*. -- I hope I see Her Highness well. Pardon this little *brusquerie*, I pray. The southern air is kind to loveliness: I regret to bring with me Her Highness's recall."

She replied in the same courteous air, inquired concerning her acquaintance, and ordered lights, -- took the letter he brought, and held it, still sealed, in the taper's flame till it fell in ashes.

"Signor," she said, lifting the white atoms of dust and sifting them through her fingers, "you may carry back these as my reply."

"Nay, I do not return," he answered. "And, Signorina, many things are pardoned to one in -- your condition. Recover your senses, and you will find this so among others."

Then, as coolly as if nothing had happened, he spoke of the affairs of the day, the tendency of measures, the feeling of the people, and finally rose, kissed her hand, and departed. He was joined without by the little Viennois, and the accursed couple sauntered down the street together. I should have gone then, -- the place was no longer safe for me, -- but something, the old spell, yet detained me.

Lenore did not speak, but threw open all the windows and doors that were closed.

"Let us be purified of his presence, at least!" she cried, when this was done.

"And you have ceased to fear this man whom you have dared so offend?" I asked.

"He is not offended," said Lenore. "Austria is not Naples. He will not transmit my reply till he is utterly past hope."

"Hope of what?"

"Of my hand."

"Lenore! Then put him beyond hope now! Become my wife!"

"Ah, -- if it were less unwise" --

"If you loved me, Lenore, you would not think of that."

"And you doubt it? Why should I, then, say again that I love you, -- I love you?"

Ah, friend, how can I repeat those words? Never have I given her endearments again to the air: sacred were they then, sacred now, however false. Ah, passionate words! oh, sweet *issimos*! tender intonations! how deeply, how deeply ye lie in my soul! Let me repeat but one sentence: it was the key to my destiny.

"Yes, yes," she said, rising from my arms, "already I do you injury. You think oftener of me than of Italy."

It was true. I sprang to my feet and began pacing the floor, as I sought to recall any instance in which I had done less than I might for my country. The cool evening-breeze, and the bell-notes sinking through the air from distant old campaniles, soothed my tumult, and, turning, I said, --

"My devotion to you sanctifies my devotion to her. And not only for her own sake do I work, but that you, you, Lenore, may have a land where no one is your master, and where your soul may develop and become perfect."

"And those who have not such object, why do they work?"

Then first I felt that I had fallen from the heights where my companions stood. This ardent patriotism of mine was sullied, a stain of selfishness rose and blotted out my glory, others should wear the conquering crowns of this grand civic game. Oh, friend! that was sad enough, but it was inevitable. Here is where the crime came in, -- that, knowing this, I still continued as their leader, suffered them to call me Master and Saviour, and walked upon the palms they spread.

Lenore mistook my silence.

"You cannot tell me why they work?" she said. "From habit, from fear, because committed? It cannot be, then, that they are in earnest, that they are sincere, that they care a rush for this cause so holy to you. They have entered into it, as all this common people do, for the love of a new excitement, for the pleasurable mystery of conspiracy, for the self-importance and gratulation. They will scatter at the signal of danger, like mischievous boys when a gendarme comes round the corner. They will betray you at the lifting of an Austrian finger. Leave them!"

This was too much to hear in silence, -- to hear of these faithful comrades, who had endured everything, and were yet to overcome because they possessed their souls in patience, each of whom stood higher before God than I in unspotted public purity, and whose praise and love led me constantly to larger effort. At least I would make them the reparation of vindication.

"You mistrust them?" I exclaimed. "They whose souls have been tried in the furnace, who have the temper of fine steel, pliant as gold, but incorruptible as adamant, -- heroes and saints, they stand so low in your favor? Come, then, come with me now, -- for the bells have struck the hour, and shadows clothe the earth, -- come to their conclave where discovery is death, and judge if they be idle prattlers, or men who carry their lives in their hands!"

Fool! Fool! Fool! Every sound in the air cries out that word to me: the bee that wings across the tower hums it in my ear; the booming alarm-bell rings it forth; my heart, my failing heart, beats it while I speak. I would have carried a snake to the sacred ibis-nest, and thenceforth hope was hollow as an egg-shell!

She ran from the room, but, pausing in the doorway, exclaimed, --

"Remember, if you take me there, that I am no Roman patriot, -- I! I, who am of the House of Austria, that House that wears the crown of the Caesars, those Caesars who swayed the very imperial sceptre, who trailed the very imperial purple of old Rome! I endure the cause because it is yours. I beseech you to be faithful to it; because I should despise you, if for any woman you swerved from an object that had previously been with you holier than heaven!"

I stood there leaning from the lofty window and looking down over the wide, solitary fields. Recollections crowded upon me, hopes rose before me. One day, that yet lives in my heart, Anselmo, sprang up afresh, a day forever domed in memory. Fair rose the sun that day, and I walked on the nation's errands through the streets of a distant town, -- a hoar and antique place, that sheltered me safely, so slight guard was it thought to need by our oppressors. It pleased that reverend arch-hypocrite to take at this hour his airing. Late events had given the people courage. It was a market-day, peasants from the country obstructed the ancient streets, the citizens were all abroad. Not few were the maledictions muttered over a column of French infantry that wound along as it returned to Rome from some movement of subjection, not low the curses showered on an officer who escorted ladies upon their drive. As I went, I considered what a day it would have been for *emeute*, and what mortal injury *emeute* would have done our cause. Italy, we said, like fools, but honest fools, must not be redeemed with blood. As if there were ever any sacred pact, any new order of things, that was not first sealed by blood! Therefore, when I, alone perhaps of all the throng, saw one man -- a man in whose soul I knew the iron rankled -- stealing behind the crowd, behind the monuments, and, as the coach of His Excellency rolled luxuriously along, levelling a glittering barrel, -- it was but an instant's work to seize the advancing creatures, to hold them rearing, -- and then a deadly flash, -- while the ball whistled past me, grazed my hand, and pierced the leader's heart. In a twinkling the dead horse was cut away, and His Excellency, cowering in the bottom of the coach, galloped home more swiftly than the wind, without a word. But the populace appreciated the action, took it up with *vivas* long and loud, that rang after me when I had slipped away, and before nightfall had echoed in all ears through leagues of country round. I went that night to the theatre. The house was filled, and, as we entered, a murmur went about, and then cries broke forth, -- the multitude rose with cheers and bravos, calling my name, intoxicated with enthusiasm, and dazzled, not by a daring feat, but by the spirit that prompted it. Women tore off their jewels to twist them into a sling for my injured hand; men rose and made me a conqueror's ovation; the orchestra played the old Etrurian hymns of freedom; I was attended home with a more than Roman triumph of torch and song, stately men and beautiful women. But chameleons change their tint in the sunshine, and why should men always march under one color? Friend, not six months later there came another day, when triumph was shame, -- plaudits, curses, -- joyous tumult, scorching silence. Oh! -- -- - But I shall come to that in time. Now let me hasten; the hours are less tardy than I, and they bring with them my last.

Thought of this day -- sole pageant defiling through memory -- was startled again by the far, sweet sound of a bell, some bell ringing twilight out and evening in across the wide Campagna. I wondered what delayed Lenore. Did it take so long to toss off the cloudy back-falling veil, to wrap in any long cloak her gown of white damask and all the sheen of her milky pearl-clusters and fiery rubies? I thought with exultation then of what she was so soon to see, -- of the route through sunken ruins, down wells forsaken of their pristine sources and hidden by masses of moss, winding with the faint light in our hands through the awful ways and avenues of the catacombs. The scene grew real to me, as I mused. Alone, what should I fear? These silent hosts encamped around would but have cheered their child. But with her, every murmur becomes a portent of danger, every current of air gives me fresh tremors; as we pass casual openings into the sky, the vault of air, the glint of stars, shall seem a malignant face; I fancy to hear impossible footsteps behind us, some bone that crumbling falls from its shelf makes my heart beat high, her dear hand trembles in my hold, and, full of a new and superstitious awe, I half fear this ancient population of the graves will rise and surround us with phantom array. Now and then, a cold, lonely wind, blowing from no one knows where, rises and careers past us, piercing to the marrow. I think, too, of that underground space, half choked with rubbish, into which we are to emerge at last, once the hall of some old Roman revel. I see the troubled flashes flung from the flaring torch over our assembly. Alert and startled, I see Lenore listen to the names as if they summoned the wraiths and not the bodies of men whom she had supposed to be lost in the pampas of Paraguay, dead in the Papal prisons, sheltered in English homes, or tossing far away on the long voyages of the Pacific seas. I see myself at length taking the torch from its niche and restoring it, as a hundred times before, to

Pietro da Valambo, while it glitters on some strange object looking in at the vine-clad opening above with its breaths of air, serpent or hare, or the large face and slow eyes of a browsing buffalo. And as I think, lo! an echo in the house, a dull tramp in the hall, a stealthy tread in the room, a heavy hand upon my shoulder, -- I was arrested for high treason.

Do not think I surrendered then. Without a struggle I would be the prize of Pope nor King nor Kaiser! I shook the minions' grasp from my shoulder, I flashed my sword in their eyes; and not till the crescent of weapons encircled me in one blinding gleam, vain grew defence, vain honor, vain bravery. Of what use was my soul to me thenceforth? I became but carrion prey. I fell, and the world fell from me.

Sensation, emotion, awoke from their swooning lapse only in the light of day, the next or another, I knew not which. I was lifted from some conveyance, I saw blue reaches of curving bay and the great purifying priest of flame, and knew I was in the city guarded by its pillar of cloud by day, of fire by night. I had reason to know it, when, yet unfed, unrested, faint, smirched and smeared with blood and travel, loaded with chains, I was brought to a tribunal where sat the sleek and subtle tyrant of Naples.

"Signor," said a bland voice from the king's side, -- and looking in its direction, I encountered the Neapolitan, -- "Signor, I lately said that at some day I would trouble you to repeat a brilliant sentence addressed to me. The day has arrived. I scarcely dared dream it would be so soon. Shall we listen?"

I was silent: not that I feared to say it; they could but finish their play.

Then I saw the beautifully cut lips of my judge part, that the voice might slide forth, and, taking a comfit, he uttered, with unchanging tint and sweetest tone, the three words, "Apply the question."

Why should I endure that for a whim? Who courts torment? Already they drew near with the cunning instruments. Let me say it, and what then? Nothing worse than torture. Let me *not* say it, and certainly torture. Oh, I was weaker than a child! my body ruled my spirit with its exhaustion and pain. Yet there was a certain satisfaction in flinging the words in their faces. I waved back with my remaining arm the slaves who approached.

"You should allow a weary man the time to collect his thoughts," I said, and then turned to my persecutors. "I have spoken with you many times, Signor," I replied to the Neapolitan, "yet of all our words I can remember none but these, that you could care to hear with this auditory. I said, -- that the tyrant of Naples walks in blood to his knees!"

The Neapolitan smiled. The king rose.

"Well said!" he murmured, in his silvery tones. "One that knows so much must know more. Exhaust his knowledge, I pray. Do not spare your courtesies; remember he is my guest. I leave him in your hands."

He fixed me with his eye, -- that darkly-glazed eye, devoid of life, of love, of joy, as if he were the thing of another element, -- then bowed and passed away.

"The urbanity of His Majesty is too well known to suppose it possible that he should prove you a liar," said the Neapolitan.

Truly, I was left in their hands! Shall I tell you of the charities I found there? Not I, friend! it would wring your heart as dry of tears as mine was wrung of groans. At last I was alone, it seemed, -- on a wet stone floor, sweat pouring from every muscle, each fibre quivering; I was distorted and unjointed, I only hoped I was dying. But no, that was too good for me. Anselmo, how can I but be full of scoffs, when I remember those hours, those ages? The cold dampness of the place crept into my bones; I became swollen and teeming with intimate pain. But that was light, my body might have ached till the throbs stiffened into death-spasms, and yet the suffering had been nought, compared with that loathing and disgust in my soul. It had seemed that I was alone, I said. Alone as the corpse in unshrouded grave! I was in a charnel-house. Men who were sinless as you hung dead upon the wall, hung dying there. Darkness covered all things at a distance, sighs crept up from far corners, chains clanked, or imprecations or prayers uttered themselves, -- bodiless voices in the night. I did not know what untold horror there might yet be hid. I heard the drip of water from the black vaults; I heart the short, fierce pants and deadly groans. Oh, worst infliction of Hell's armory it is to see another suffer! Why was it allowed, Anselmo? Did it come in the long train of a broken law? was it one of the dark places of Providence? or was it indeed the vile compost to mature some beautiful germ? Ah, then, is it possible that Heaven looks on us so in the mass?

But for me, after a while I lay torpid, and then perchance I slept, for finally I opened my eyes and found the white strong light; I lay on a bed, and a surgeon handled me. Too elastic was I to be long crushed, once the weight removed. Soon I breathed fresh air; and save that my frame had become in its distortion hideous, I was the same as before.

Then, indeed, began my torture, -- torture to which this had been idle jest. I was taken once more to the room of tribunal. Beside the Neapolitan a woman sat veiled and shrouded in masses of sable drapery. "A queen?" I thought, "or a slave?" But I had no further room for fancy; the same interrogatories as before were given me to answer, and then I felt why I had been nursed back to life. In the months that had elapsed, I could not know if Italy were saved or lost, if Naples tottered or remained impregnable. I stood only on my personal basis of right or wrong. I refused to open my lips. They wheeled forward a low bed that I knew well. Oh, the slow starting of the socket! Oh, the long wrench of tendon and nerve! A bed of steel and cords, rollers and levers, bound me there, and bent to their creaking toil. I was strong to endure; I had set my teeth and sworn myself to silence; no woman should hear me moan. Even in this misery I saw that she who sat there, shaking, fell.

The tyrant was lily-livered; seldom he witnessed what others died under; he intended nothing further then; -- many men who faint at sight of blood can probe a soul to its utmost gasp. Now he motioned, and they paused. Then others lifted the woman and held her beside him, yet a little in advance.

"Keep your silence," said he, in a voice unrecognizable, and as if a wild beast, half-glutted, should speak, "and I keep her! She is in my power. Mine, and you know what that means. Mine," and he bent toward me, " *body -- and -- soul*. To use, to blast, to destroy, to tear piecemeal, -- as I will do, so help me God! unless you meet my condition." And extending his hand, he drew aside the black veil, and my eye lay on the face of Lenore, thin and white as the familiar faces of corpses, and utterly insensible in swoon.

Ah, that mortal horror stops my pulse! Was I wrong? Why not have borne that, too? Had she loved me, she had chosen it, chosen it rather. And death would have made all right! -- God! why not have seized some poignard lying there? why not have sprung upon her, have slain her? Then silence had been simply secure. Then I could have smiled in their frustrated faces, one keen, deep smile, and died. I was dissolved in pain, writhed with prolonged strokes that thrilled me from head to foot, pierced as with acute stabs, my heart seemed to forge thunderbolts to break upon my brain, -- but this agony had been spared me. They unbound me, fed me with some stimulating cordial, gave me cold air, and I rose on my elbow a little.

"Swear!" I said, hoarsely. "But you do not keep oaths. God help you? Never! There must be a Hell to help you! Imprecate this, then, on yourself. May you in your smooth white body know the torture I have known, be racked till each bone in your skin changes place, hang festering in chains from the wall of a living grave, make fellowship with putridity, and lie in the pitiless dark to see all the dead who died under your hand rise, rise and accuse you before God! And may your little son know the deeds you have done, live the life those deeds merit, and die the death that *I* shall die, -- if you do not keep your word!"

"What word?" he said.

"Promise, if I reveal all, and my revelations shall be true and thorough therefore, -- promise that you will leave her in safe security and freedom to-day, untouched, unscathed, unharmed, and that so ever shall she remain. And false to this oath, may no priest shrive you, no land own you, God blight you and curse you and wither you from the face of the earth!"

And taking a crucifix, he swore the oath.

Then they busied themselves about Lenore, revived her, soothed her, gave her of the same cordial to drink, and placed her once more in her dais-seat. Her veil was thrown back, her wide blue eyes fixed on me in intense strain, her face and lips still blanched more bitterly beneath that hue, her features sharp as chisel-graven death. Ah, God! must I endure that too? Was she to hear me, -- she, not knowing why, never knowing why, -- she in whom that look of aching passion and pity was to die out and freeze and fade in one of utter scorn?

They brought me some strange draught, as if one swallowed fire. The blood coursed richly through my shrunken veins; I felt filled with a different life. I arose and left that bed of torture, but came back to it as to my rest.

And lying there, I betrayed Italy.

Root and branch and spray and leaf, I uprooted all my memories; I forgot no name, I lost no fact; I was eagerer than they; I modified nothing, I abbreviated nothing; the past, the future, what had been, was to be, plan and scheme and supreme purpose, I never faltered, I told the whole!

I did not look at her, I kept my eyes on the tyrant; I wished I might have the evil eye, -- but that gift was for him, the Neapolitan. Yet at length I heard a low moan trailing toward me; I turned and saw her face, as I saw it last, Anselmo, -- stonily quiet, frozen from indignant pain to icy apathy, and the words she would have said had hissed inarticulately through her ashen lips. Then they brought me the confession, and, as I could, I signed it.

"Madame," said the tyrant, "your knowledge is coextensive with his. Does all this agree?"

"Sire, it does agree," she answered, and they led her out.

"I have no authority over you," said the tyrant then to me. "You might go freely now, but that, precious as Homer, seven cities claim you, Signor! My prisons also will now be full of rarer game. But as a crime of your commission places you within Austrian jurisdiction, I shall take pleasure in presenting you to my cousin and surrendering you to his mercy," and he withdrew.

"You may not be aware," said the courteous Neapolitan, "that on the night of your arrest your frantic sword-slashes had serious result. My friend the little Viennois fell at your hands."

"God be praised," I answered, "that I do not die without one good work!"

"Well said! And worthy of a traitor both to his ancient blood and to his cause, -- the betrayer of comrade and friend!"

I do not know what look was in my eye, or whether, with the savage ferocity taught me but now, I was about to leap and throttle him, and suck the life-blood from his veins. But suddenly he laughed, a feigned merriment, twirled his moustache, opened a door, looked back, uttering this one sentence: --

"You have simply corroborated her statement: you are not even the first in at the death: Lenore told all this more swiftly, with a better grace, and a something less sardonic mute-comment," -- closed the door and was gone. The breath of the bottomless pit had blown in my face.

They gave themselves time to swoop down and pounce on every man whose name I had given, and others; they prevented future trouble, they made terrible examples, they sated themselves with vengeance. But their feet were shod with velvet, -- history will never record it; to the world I and those nameless ones pass as mere idle agitators, bubbles that blew out to sea, -- but at my mention kings in their closet remember how their thrones trembled! Then they looked about them for one last morsel, and I was led to Rome.

O stormy days that I have to remember! O wild mornings of the cannonade, and of the sally! One noon blots ye all out in sullen darkness!

It was a gala-day, the day when I passed through; all the populace were out, my signed confession placarded the corners, Pasquin harvested my sins, Church and State made holiday. Cries of derision awaited me, ribald laughter, taunting jests, hisses and groans, gleaming stilettos, shining barrels, eyes of rage. But when I reached them, all was silence; silence closed up the ranks behind me. The shouting crowds grew noiseless, breathless. They each received the terrible impress of him who passed, -- his brow was branded as by doom; he went out Cain, and carried with him the curse of a ruined people. I gazed right and left, -- on these men who had once hailed me, followed me, worshipped me; their hate melted as they met my eye; slowly a cloud of terror and pity gathered and hung above the city. I did not repent; I would have done it again: not for a universe of Italies would I have resigned *her* to that fate. But, O friend, this forgiveness of theirs was unmerciful! For hate they had cause; for this none: they knew nothing of my reason, they only knew that I had betrayed them. Each man had despised me; he thought that to save my limbs like a young god's, to keep my face that had been splendid in youth's beauty, to spare that shape of antique symmetry and grace, to win ease and rest and wealth and happiness, perhaps, I had done this. Each man, as I met his gaze, shrunken, dismembered, deformed, dishonored, held his breath, shook with indefinable fear, felt the neighborhood of agony and despair, and forgave, forgave: -- oh! to live to be forgiven! But the women, -- the women, Anselmo, were not so cruel. There were torrents of streamers, but all were black, pouring from window and roof, -- there were sunny heads, and dark, fair faces, rosy cheeks, snowy shoulders, clustered in door and arch like bunches of poison-flowers, -- and of all shrill sounds of hate, Anselmo, that can pierce and part red lips, the fiercest, shrillest, fell on me; and at last, from one lofty balcony, where erst I had seen her leaning forth in sunset to catch the evening winds, the evening bells, crowned, too, by the evening star, one woman, now centred in merciless mid-noon, leaned, leaned and gazed down as into her grave: it was Lenore. It had been late spring when last I passed that way; all the hot, pestilential summer I had lain in the dungeons of Naples; now it was autumn, and the town was full. Full, but I saw no one; blank became the spaces on which I gazed; my gyves vanished, my guards; my brain swam through dazzling rings of light, and I fell forward in the cart and hung by my chains among the hoofs of the trampling horses who dragged me. On that day I had taken my last step; I never set foot on the round earth again. But, with all, I smiled through my groans; for the shining, solid hoofs that did their work on me did their work as well on the man who walked by my side, -- dashed dead the accursed Neapolitan.

They were not the surgeons of Naples who essayed to galvanize volition through my paralyzed limbs, but those who knew the utmost resources of their art. And so I lived, -- lived, too, by reason of my inextinguishable vitality, by reason of this spark that will not quench, -- and so I came to Hellberg. It would have been mockery to give this shapeless hulk to sentence, and then to headsman or hangman; perhaps, too, her haughty name had been involved; and so I was never brought to trial, and so I am at Hellberg.

And I have never set foot on the ground again. But, oh, to touch it for a moment, to sit anywhere on the summer mould, to pull down the sun-quivering, sun-steeped branches about me, to scent the fresh grass as it springs to the light! Oh, but to touch the sweet, kind earth, the warm earth, silent with ineffable tenderness and soothing, to feel it under my hand, to lay my cheek there for a moment, while it drew away pain and weariness with its absorbing, purifying power! Oh, but to lie once more where the blossoms grow! Soon, soon, they will grow above me! Soon the kind mother will cover me!

What had happened in the outer world I knew not till you came. I fancied Lenore returned, breathing Austrian air, and living under the same horizon that girds me in. Sometimes I have seen a distant cavalcade skimming over the vale, as once we careered over the Campagna, when she handled her steed as another woman handles her needle, and the sweet wind fanned peach-tints to her cheeks and drew out unravelled braids of gold in lingering caress. She could have come to me, had she pleased, then: this old chief who rules the place was her father's friend and hers. -- But look! but see! Who is it comes now, -- sweeps round the donjon flank? Lean over the embrasure, and learn! Ah, man, are my eyes so old, my memories so treacherous, that I do not know day from night? They have gone on, -- or did they enter, think you? Or yet, there is to be carousal, perhaps, in the halls beyond and below, and she comes to join the gay feast; she will drink healths in red wine, will listen to flattering dalliance with pleased eyes, will utter light laughs through the lips that once glowed to my kisses, and will forget that the same roof which shelters the revellers shelters also her lover dying in moans? Careless - - -- - Best so! best so! What cavalier whispered in her ear as she passed? Have years tarnished her beauty? Ah, God! this wind, that maddens me now, a moment since touched her!

Anselmo, I will go in. This vault of heaven with its spotless blue, this wide land that laughs in festive summer, these winds that lift my hair and come heavy with odors, -- these do not fit with me, I burlesque the fair face of creation. O invisible airs, that softly sport round the castle-towers, why do you not woo my soul forth and bear it and lose it in the flawless cope of sky?

Nay, why, any more than Ajax, should I die in the dark? Never again will I enter the cell, never again! The wide universe shall receive my breath. Lower the back of my chair, pull away the cushions, wrap my cloak round me, Anselmo. There! I will lie, and wait, and look up. Give me ghostly counsel, my friend, console me. You are not too weary with this long tale? Tell me I needed all the tears I have shed to quench the fiery defiance, the independence of heaven and tumult of earth in my being. If you could tell me that she had not been false, that she never feigned her passion to decoy, that, Austrian though she were -- --- - Ah, but I had evidence! I had evidence! his words, that ate out my life like gangrene and rust. -- Speak slower, Anselmo, slower. Can it be that I sinned most, when I held his words before hers, -- his black damning falsehoods? -- Mother of God! do you know what you say?

Tell me, then, that I am a fool, -- that not through other loss than the loss of faith did the curse fall on me! Tell me, then, that these dark ways lead me out on a height! Needful the shadow and the groping. He anointed my eyes with the clay beneath his feet, -- I was blind, but now I see God!

Repeat, Anselmo, repeat that she was true, though the knowledge blast me with self-consuming pangs. But, true or false, one thing she promised me: though other spheres, though other lives had come between us, she would be with me in my dying hour. Soon the bell will toll that hour, and toll my knell!

What is this, Anselmo, -- this face that hangs between me and heaven, -- this pitying, sorrowing countenance? -- Ave Maria! -- Never! Never! Still of the earth, this melting mouth, these violet eyes, this brow of snow, this fragrant bosom pillowing my head! Mirage of fainting fancy, -- out, beautiful thing, away! Do not torment me with such a despairing lie! do not cheat me into death! let me at least look on the unobstructed sky, as I sink lower and lower to my eternal rest!

Still there? Still there? Still bending above me, smiling and weeping, sweet April face? Oh, were they truly thy lips that lay on mine, then, that stamped them with life's impress, that woke me? Are they truly thy fingers that pressed my throbless temples? These arms that are wound about me, are thine? Thy heart beats for me, thy tears flow, thy perfect womanhood does not recoil in horror? Lenore! Lenore! is it thou?

Nay, nay, Sweet, ask me no question; I have wronged thee; he shall tell thee how. Yet best thou shouldst never hear it. Sin to thee greater than all treachery had been. Forgive, forgive! I go, -- in meeting, leave thee; but be glad for me, -- whether I sleep or whether I wake, know that a great curse will have fallen from me. Swathe my memory in thy love. Kiss me again, child! Rock me a little; stoop lower, and croon those old mountain-songs that once you sang when the sunshine soaked the sward and your hair was crowned with blue morning-glories.

Ah, your song drowns in tears! Yet you do not wish me to live, Lenore? O love, I can do nothing but die!

The sunlight fades from the hills, the air wavers and glimmers, and day is dim. Thy face is mistier than a vision of angels. There are faint, strange voices in my ear, swift rustlings, far harmonies; -- has sense become so attenuated that I hear the blood in my failing pulses? Lenore, love, lower. Thy lips to mine, and breathe my life away. Twice would I die to save thee!

-- Anselmo! man! where art thou? Come back ere I fall, -- strength flares up like a dying flame. *Never tell her why I betrayed Italy!*

-- Closer, dear love, closer! What old murmurs do I hear?

"The night is spread for thee,
The heavens are wide,
And the dark earth's mystery" --

So, -- in thy arms, -- from thee to God! O love, forever -- kiss -- forgive! -- Life me, that I confront eternity and Christ!

www.ingramcontent.com/pod-product-compliance
Lightning Source LLC
Chambersburg PA
CBHW020919180626
46816CB00007BA/2474